Dara

Autobiography of a
Chesapeake Bay Retriever

Dara

Autobiography of a
Chesapeake Bay Retriever

transcribed by Lolo Sarnoff
drawings by Cole Johnson
photographs by Linda Rosenthal

Posterity Press, Inc.
Chevy Chase, Maryland

Posterity Press, Inc.,
PO Box 71081
Chevy Chase,
Maryland 20813
ISBN 1-889274-06-2

Sarnoff, Lolo
    Dara: The Autobiography of a Chesapeake Bay Retriever
    Transcribed by Lolo Sarnoff
        p.   cm.
    ISBN 1-88974-06-2
    1. Chesapeake Bay Retrievers Fiction. 2. Dogs Fiction
I. Title.
PS3569.A695D37 1999   99-13016
813'.54--dc21   CIP

Dedication

THIS BOOK IS DEDICATED TO DARA'S CANINE FOUNATION, INC., my recently established 501(c) (3) not-for-profit organization. Proceeds from my book are for the benefit of this foundation, which will financially assist animal shelters' adoption programs and thereby, hopefully, prolong the lives of my less fortunate fellow dogs.

Acknowledgment

USUALLY THE AUTHOR HAS TO THANK MANY ASSISTANTS. I ONLY want to thank one—my Mom. She understood my thoughts and transcribed them for me. I also want to thank her for adopting me despite my difficult character and my many bad habits. Mom realized immediately that I have a generous and loving soul.

—Dara

Transcriber's Note

MARRIED FOR 43 YEARS, MY HUSBAND AND I SHARED THE LAST 11 years of his life with a beautiful Rottweiler lady. I have to call her a lady, as she was really ladylike in her behavior. Koka and I spent one more year together, just the two of us, and became even closer. I nearly forgot that I was lonely. Then suddenly one evening, eight years ago, she felt very uneasy. I took her into my arms and she stopped breathing.

For two weeks, I got lonelier and lonelier. Even in my grief, I knew I had to get another dog. So a friend and I took off to the animal shelter, where I described the dog I was looking for: small, well-trained, housebroken, healthy — with a happy childhood — if possible, and black. "Of course," the director told me, "I know just what you are looking for." We passed at least 30 nice small- and medium-sized dogs; I was not allowed to look at any of them. Finally, we arrived at a cage just slightly out of the way. After it was opened, out jumped a very large brown dog, definitely a hunter — a Chesapeake Bay Retriever. On the leash, she pulled the director to a lying position. She was the total opposite to what I had been looking for. However, I saw a big black "X" on her cage. Inquiring what that meant, I found that it was her death sentence. I was told by the director that I was her last hope of saving this beautiful thoroughbred dog. What was I to do?

—*Lolo Sarnoff*

Prologue

I AM A CHESAPEAKE BAY RETRIEVER, HIGHLY BRED WITH A LONG pedigree and very fancy ancestors. I am also a shelter dog. My present name is Dara; however, I was born and registered as Kara. My life can only be compared to a roller coaster ride, with ups and downs from very high to very low to high again.

I am actually a very private individual. I do not like to talk about myself, but so many unusual things have happened to me that I must. I am not really a "do-gooder," as I am very selfish. However, I want to help other dogs who were caught on the street without a home, just as it happened to me. I have decided to write my autobiography hopefully to earn some money. I will give all the royalties I might receive from this book to the charitable foundation I have created. I want to rebuild the animal shelter I stayed in, and build large runs there for all its dog guests, so they no longer have to pass so much of their time in cages.

I am a very large dog. When I was at the shelter, my cage was much too small. Most of all I had nothing to do except a ten-minute walk in the morning, at noon and in the evening. Sometimes a young and helpful girl took me out and played with me and gave me some very much needed exercise. She even brought me a toy to play with. Her visit was the highlight of each week. If I could raise enough money, the shelter could hire people to play with the dogs, walk them and help them find homes—not a bad job after all.

My new Mom runs something she calls a "not-for-profit organization." I asked her if dogs could create a "not-for-profit organization." She decided it might be possible—unusual, but she likes unusual things. So we created Dara's Canine Foundation, Inc. I am the Vice President and my Mom is the Chairman of the Board. We also have a Treasurer, but no treasure yet.

Now you understand why I had to write my autobiography and I hope you will enjoy reading it. Maybe you will buy an extra copy of my book for a friend. With your help, I will not only rebuild the animal shelter which found my new Mom for me, but as many other shelters as my money will allow.

At another shelter near where we live, I saw a lot of teenagers who were helping there. To help in a shelter is a good job for a young person after school and on weekends, much better than getting into mischief.

My book will try to tell you what dogs think and why we do some things and why we don't do everything we are expected to do. Many of you believe that the only way to communicate with us is by saying, "Sit, stay, down, come, food, bed," and the few other words you use with us. This is not true at all. We enjoy it when you talk to us. We often try to answer, hoping that you will understand us. Dogs think, dogs have a lot of feelings. Just like humans. Dogs like to excel. Dogs love to be praised, and dogs like to be loved, especially me. I never get tired of hearing that I am beautiful and intelligent, even if I know it already.

Are you curious about my three lives? The wonderful first one when I was Kara, the ghastly one as Brownie, and now my present life as Dara, the dog who dreams about helping other dogs.

Chapter 1

MY DOG MUMMY TOLD ME THAT IT WAS A BEAUTIFUL CLEAR night when I was born, whatever that might mean. When I arrived, there were already four little creatures squirming around, whimpering, not knowing exactly what to do, just like me. Shortly after me, one more little creature appeared, landing on top of me. Mummy cleaned us up and arranged us on a blanket. The first thing she taught us was how to find one of her nipples and how to suck, not easy when you've never had to do anything yourself, especially eat. When one is born, everything changes. At first, we could not even see where we were. But Mummy assured us that this would not last long, and it didn't.

When we were all full and were taking a rest, some two-legged creatures appeared. They went into screams of joy at seeing the six of us. They were saying how beautiful we were and how clever Mummy was to have given birth to all of us alone, without any help—as if she needed help from these two-legged creatures who seem to think they know everything better. The first thing these creatures—humans—decided to do was to put us in a large box, probably to keep track of us. Thank heavens we didn't have to stay there long. Mummy came and went to nurse us, to lick us and to comfort us.

Life became more interesting every day. Four of my siblings were grabby, always pushing and shoving, always wanting to get the best tit. But there was one special brother, the one born just after me. I immediately liked him best. We stayed together and played together, trying to ignore the other four. When we got older, the humans let us play in the yard. It was all fenced in so we couldn't get lost. It was big, with lots of interesting smells. We discovered a new world we enjoyed immensely.

Then we all got names. I was Kara; my favorite brother was Karim. One sister was Katie. I forget the names of the others. However, every name started with the same sound. We grew and grew and learned to eat out of a bowl. After several weeks, new humans came. They admired us, and then took one of the others with them. I never saw them again.

Nobody could pick me or Karim. The lady we lived with—I called her "Mother"—had decided that Karim and I were going to stay with her. She probably chose us because we were the most beautiful and the smartest. Our Mummy lived with us also. She was called Georgie. She was the favorite of "Dad." I never met my dog father as he did not live with us. I might have seen him at a big duck shoot later, but, if I did, no one told me who he was. If he was there, he took no notice of Karim or me. Probably he did not recognize us. Dog fathers do not take care of their offspring. They leave this to the mummies and the humans. So we dogs love our human families more than we love other dogs, except for me. I loved Karim as much as Mother. When dogs lose our human families, as I did, we become very morose.

Lots of humans lived with me. Aside from Mother and Dad, there were two sons, Peter and Michael; the cook; the maid; Freddy, who looked after the horses; and all kinds of people looking after the garden, the cows and the chickens.

One morning, Mother decided that we were old enough to have the run of the whole house. We no longer had to stay only in the kitchen. The first thing she taught us was that nice little dogs do not mess up a house. That seemed logical. It did not take Karim and me long to catch on. At first we got a little reward, like a cookie, if we did not dirty the house. Soon we were expected to be housebroken, and we were.

We each received a collar with a tag. It had our name, telephone number and address engraved on it, in case we got lost. But why would we get lost? We were living in the most beautiful place, Trinity Hall. There was endless space to roam around in. Our humans who owned it were wonderful and loved us, and we loved all of them, especially Mother.

Karim and I were always together. We never did anything alone. We liked to explore; sometimes we stayed away longer than we were supposed to. When we did, Mother got all excited and we were punished and had to stay in the yard.

We were living very close to a large water, called the Chesapeake Bay. It did not take us long to discover it. At first, we only waded, then we started swimming which was delicious. We were soon very fast swimmers. Life was wonderful.

We each had our own bed, although Karim and I preferred to sleep together, sometimes in his bed, sometimes in mine. As we grew older and stronger. Mother was not as concerned that we would get lost. She took us often in her car for rides. We met her horse, Filou, and we were allowed to run along when she rode, which she did nearly every day.

At Trinity Hall, all the neighbors seemed to know and like each other. It was hard to tell where our land ended and theirs started. Everybody we met remarked that Karim and I were unusually beautiful Chesapeake Bay Retrievers. We are the rare kind with red-brown fur and lots of curls, all in the right places. We have yellow eyes and narrow heads, and we are tall and slender.

Mother took us for many beautiful drives. But one day we stopped at a place with a horrid smell. It didn't seem to be the right place to visit, but we were on the leash and had no choice. It was the veterinarian. He tried to be friendly and told us how beautiful we were and gave us each a cookie. But then the examination started. It was not so bad until, suddenly, he gave us all kinds of pokes. They were injections. It did not really hurt; nevertheless, I whimpered. I did not like it. I made up my mind that I was not ever going to return there, cookie or no cookie. Famous thoughts!

Chapter 2

We GREW AND GREW AND GOT TO BE STRONGER AND MORE playful and even faster swimmers. One day we discovered ducks. What fun it was to chase them! Dad decided that it was time to train us as duck retrievers. He told us we were going to get lessons from a man named Jack.

Jack came every day. He promised to turn us into the best retrievers on the Bay and he did. He could tell that we were quick learners and very smart. He taught us how to retrieve, although retrieving is in our blood. By our nature, we do not hurt what we retrieve. First he threw sticks into the water. We had to bring them back to him on the shore, never biting them. Then he threw a wooden something with a duck smell and we did the same thing. Soon we knew how to retrieve without hurting the thing with the duck smell, some kind of "decoy." Then he fired a gun—a lot. We got used to this new noise, and learned to go into the water only after it stopped.

We also learned to swim quickly toward real ducks and to chase them so they flew in the direction of Jack. We were not allowed to touch them, just to swim near to them and chase them. We never touched one. He seemed pleased with our performance. We made a few mistakes, but we learned quickly. We loved it and felt very important.

One day Dad told us he was taking Karim and me and our Mummy Georgie to our first duck shoot. His sons Peter and Michael would come along. They were pretty big; but they still had to go to school, so I guess they were not very old. We went in Dad's plane. Since there was room we were allowed to sit on a seat and look out the window; however, no barking or running around. We had to sit still. We were well behaved and sat in our seats like a perfect lady and gentleman. I loved the plane. I still adore to fly in a plane.

The day of the duck shoot we flew to a friend's property where we were introduced to some other Chessies who had hunted before. It was fall and the water was already cold, but I love cold water, so that did not faze me at all. By now we were nearly grown and very strong.

I have to tell you what happened at the hunt. There were many men and a few women. Mother did not come along. She did not seem to like hunting or maybe it was the shooting. Jack came with us. He told us that for the first time we were at a real duck shoot and that we had to be very attentive and follow his commands. There were a lot of ducks in the sky flying in the direction of some decoys which had been put up near the hunters who were hidden in blinds.

There was a lot of shooting. Many ducks fell in the water. When the shooting stopped, we were let loose to retrieve real ducks. We remembered not to hurt the ducks. We brought them to the beach and lined them up, until there were none left in the water. The hunters left the blinds and inspected the ducks. There were many. Karim and I got a lot of compliments.

After gathering the ducks in the plane, we flew home. Mother had arranged a party. The hunters went to the living room. They all had drinks, they seemed very happy, and they congratulated each other. They really should have congratulated us, but they congratulated themselves, "What wonderful shots they were!" and they celebrated all evening whilst we were lying in front of the fire. It had been a great day.

One duck shoot followed the other. Sometimes the shoot was on our estate, sometimes we flew to somebody else's and other times we drove; it depended on the distance. It was always fun and we always came back with many ducks. Sometimes the ducks were geese. Geese are so much like ducks that I had difficulty telling the difference. However, when geese get excited, they make a different noise than ducks, and they fly in a special formation.

When it was a goose shoot, we retrieved geese. Very carefully, very gently I brought a goose to the shore, then the second, then the third, at least six. (You know I can count to ten.) I'm sure Karim did as well. Georgie was an old hand at it. I know she did well.

The humans decided to go to another blind quite far away, and the hunting and shooting started all over. The second time I got seven geese, which is very unusual, a record for me. The humans must have been very good shots, or I was a very good retriever. Maybe both.

Finally, the humans were cold and had had enough. They were banging their arms around and jumping up and down. As usual they were very pleased with themselves. They collected all the geese and put them in a special section of the cars. We piled in, the humans piled in, and we drove home and had another party.

Chapter 3

I T WAS A WONDERFUL FALL AND EARLY WINTER. WHEN THE SNOW started to fall we played in it. Karim and I did not have many responsibilities, only to guard the house, the cars and the plane, when needed. We would never let anyone we did not know come near the house. We both had great teeth. Strangers thought we would bite them, but we would not do that. We only made our position clear by showing our teeth and growling.

Apart from guarding the house, we guarded Mother wherever she went. We had a perfect life. Cook took care of our meals, there was always fresh water, our beds were clean, everybody made a great fuss about Karim and me.

It got colder and colder; the pond froze, as well as part of the Bay. Often the snow stayed on the ground. I cannot tell you how much fun it is to play in the snow and on the ice. Karim and I invented all kinds of lovely games. Our favorite was to see who could slide the farthest. Guess who won? When it got too cold, the duck shoots stopped, but we kept busy playing, eating, sleeping, driving in the car, flying when we got invited and running along with Filou, Mother's horse.

Mother loved to ride. Everybody rode, but Mother really loved it more than anyone else. Sometimes I was a little jealous of Filou, especially when Mother fussed too much with him. Once I got so angry I bit his hind leg. Nobody saw it. He tried to get even and kicked me. After awhile we made up and were friends again.

One morning something surprising happened. Cook discovered bloody spots on the kitchen floor, she got all excited and called Mother, who also got very excited. She locked me up in one part of the house and would not let me out. Worst of all, I was not allowed to be near Karim. He had to stay away, and we even had to go outside alone. It was horrible: nothing to do, no one to play with. In a few days I stopped spotting and Mother decided that this horrible situation could stop. Karim came back. What a relief. We were both delighted.

We continued to accompany Mother when she went riding. She nearly always took us. Now we could run as fast as Filou. If the fences he jumped were too high, we found a way around. Often we jumped too. Filou was not always nice since he was also jealous. He wanted to have Mother all for himself, and so did we. When he was in a real bad mood he kicked, then we kept out of his way, but most of the time we all got along very well. Winter passed, and spring came again.

One day Mother went riding and took neither Karim nor me. Maybe she could not find us. She did not come back. When Dad came home from work he asked where Mother was. Where was Filou? Nobody had seen them.

Then suddenly, Filou appeared by himself—without Mother. That was very strange. He had never done that before. He seemed very upset. Dad got very worried. I can't blame him. I got very worried. We all got very worried. We piled into the Rover and went where Mother might have been riding on her favorite trails. Then Karim and I got out of the car. We wanted to look for ourselves, off the road. Dad let us go; he knew we would not get lost.

We searched for Mother all over. Suddenly, I saw her lying in some bushes, all pale and not moving. Can you imagine? I had never seen Mother not moving. I started to bark like crazy, and everybody came running. When they saw Mother they picked her up very carefully and put her in the car and drove her home. She still was not moving. She still was not saying anything.

Soon a big van with flashing lights arrived and took Mother away. Dad drove away after them; nobody told us anything. Either they did not know or they did not want us to know. We got so worried that we did not even eat dinner. We just waited and waited. Finally Dad came home looking all shaken and gray. He told us that Mother had had an accident and was very ill.

He hoped that we would understand. What could we do? We licked his hands and told him we loved him. Peter and Michael were there too. They cried. Nobody wanted to go to bed. Early the next morning, the telephone rang. I do not think it was good news. Dad, Michael and Peter left and did not take us. That was unusual. We stayed at home and waited and waited and waited all day. We did not even want to play. This went on for days. I am not sure how many.

One day, they brought Mother back home. But she was not like Mother. She could not talk, she could hardly move, she had to stay in bed. Everybody was around her bed. We tried to cheer her up. We were with her constantly. We licked her hands to tell her how much we loved her. It did not make any difference. She did not move. Things went from bad to worse. There were nurses all over the place. Doctors came in and out of the house.

Weeks went by and then one day Mother could not breathe and she would not open her eyes. Dad told us, "Mother is dead." We did not know what dead was. But Mother was dead. Lots of people came to the house, many flowers arrived and lots of food. We got so upset that we barked at everybody. So we got locked up. Then some people came and took Mother away. Dead Mother. Maybe dead means that you never come back. Mother never came back. The wonderful, happy, laughing house became quiet and sad.

Chapter 4

PETER DISCUSSED WITH DAD WHAT HE WAS GOING TO DO AFTER his graduation from high school, whatever that might mean. He told Dad that he would like to go to a college in New England, that it was far away but a great school for computer science. In addition it was a school where he could take his dog along. His dog, meaning me. After Mother's death, Dad gave me to Peter and Karim to Michael. Georgie would always be Dad's special dog. For the first time Karim and I would be separated. Michael, being too young, had to continue to go to high school. Therefore Karim was not going anywhere.

I was not sure if I wanted to go to college. Why would I want to go to another school? I had been to school. I had learned how to retrieve ducks and geese. I didn't want to learn to write on a computer and read a lot of books. But humans have strange ways. They don't ask us for our opinion, they just tell us and expect us to accept their decision and be content.

Peter and Dad told me that after the summer I was going to go to college. Therefore, I should swim and play and do everything I enjoyed all summer long with Karim. Life would be different: no duck hunting, no Bay, no Karim, no freedom, no running around. It was a glorious summer, but lonesome without Mother. Maybe Georgie would get more babies, so Dad could get some more retrievers. He would never get one as loyal and beautiful as myself.

One day, Peter packed his bags. He packed a little bag for me, not that I needed very much. But he did not want to forget my favorite bowls, my favorite balls, my favorite toys and a big blanket for me to lie on. I wouldn't even have a bed in college? I do not like to sleep on the floor!

Peter piled everything into his new station wagon which he had gotten as a present for graduation. There was a nice place in the back part just for me, quite comfortable. We drove away. Dad seemed very sad. Not as sad as I was to leave him and Karim and Trinity Hall. Maybe especially to leave Karim. We had never been separated for a day since we were born except that once. How would I manage without him? Peter realized how sad I was, so he told me he would play with me, he would take me for walks, he would see that I would not get lonely. He would try his best to replace all I had to leave behind.

After a long, long drive, we arrived at the college. Peter had to look for the house where we were going to stay. He took in all the suitcases and boxes, the computer and the television. Then I was allowed to come. Everybody in the house exclaimed how beautiful I was, just a little big for a student dorm.

I was not very friendly, but I was not unfriendly either. Why should I make friends with all kinds of people I did not know, who were standing around looking at me and saying, "Who is this?" Peter introduced me. "This is Kara. She is a Chesapeake Bay Retriever. She will go to class with me. We will do everything together. She is my friend." He could have said, "She is my dog," but he was too polite to say that so he said "She is my friend."

We went to his room, and you would not believe this: he had a roommate. There was another boy. Not too much to look at but pleasant enough. He was called Fred. The three of us had to share this room. I looked around and I could not see a place where I was going to sleep. There were two beds, two chairs, two desks and a sofa. Was the sofa going to be my bed? Peter was not certain. He still had the blanket in his arm.

Well, I suppose he wanted to make friends with Fred. So he said, "Where do you think Kara should sleep?" Fred did not suggest the sofa. My blanket was put on the floor. Peter told me this was where I was going to sleep. Thank heaven there was a thick carpet on the floor so it would not be too uncomfortable. He put my two bowls out and said "This is where you are going to eat and drink."

Peter wanted to show me where he was going to go to school. Instead of unpacking, he took me for a long walk all over the campus. He showed me everything around the college, which was rather pretty. I met a few dogs, not very interesting, nobody like Karim.

When we came home I got my dinner. Peter unpacked his things, then he went out and told me I had to guard the room, which I did. I nearly didn't let Fred come in. I had forgotten that he now lived with us. I had never spent the night with a stranger. However, we all got used to each other, except Fred snored. But do you know what? Next morning, he complained to Peter that I snored! I think he must have heard himself, because I never snore.

After breakfast we walked off to class. There were ever so many boys and girls. The first thing Peter told me was that I must be very quiet and not talk during class, that I must not bark or do anything until he tells me, or I could not come back. I had no choice. I was quiet all morning.

Then we went for a walk. No swim. It was warm and I was longing for the Bay, I was longing for Karim, I was longing for home. I made up my mind that I did not like college. My Mummy Georgie had told me long ago, I remembered just in time, that we all have to make the best of things. Life is not always like we wish it to be, as she had said, "a garden filled with hot-dogs."

I was going to school because I liked Peter. I did not love him like I had loved Mother. He was trying his best to make my life pleasant. I was very homesick. I was thinking of Karim and all the lovely games we played together. I was also thinking of Dad, and I thought of Mother all the time. What if she came home when I was not there? Dad said she was dead, but I still do not know what dead is. One day, before we left for college, Dad placed a lot of flowers and a stone where Mother is now. Would Mother live under a stone? Ridiculous!

Finally, I made a friend—an Irish setter. She was not as beautiful, intelligent or lovable as Karim. But we both loved to play follow the leader, catch-catch and some other special games. She lived not too far away. We saw each other often.

Every few days Peter and I went to the woods where I could run around without a leash and follow the different scents I chose. It was a regular event that I think Peter liked as much as I did. When summer came, we packed and went home to Trinity Hall, but in the fall, we both went back to college. In the spring of that second year on one of these outings, I met a beautiful collie I liked, who also seemed to find me attractive. He taught me to play a new kind of game: he jumped all around and on me, and wouldn't let go. After a while, he just stopped and left. When Peter called me to go back to the dorm, I did not tell him about it.

When Peter finished that semester, it was time for our summer vacation. I expected him to drive me home as he had done before, except for the time at Christmas he took me skiing, which I liked. I adored cross-country skiing! However, he had a different plan: He told me that he was getting a job in a big city. I had never been to a big city. But he told me that he could not take me along, as I could not accompany him to the office where he was going to work.

Without asking me, he had decided that I would spend the vacation with his friend Josh. Why did he do that? He certainly must have known that I did not like Josh and that Josh did not like me. I still wonder why Josh agreed to take me. It was a very bad decision. Peter packed his car and drove me and my belongings to Josh's house, just outside town. He stayed for a bit and departed, telling me he would be back in September when his classes started again. He should have taken me home to Trinity Hall, but he didn't.

Josh and I hit it off very badly. I could do nothing he approved of. He constantly reprimanded me for all kinds of stupid things—like not drinking neatly enough, or wanting him to help me find my ball, which he had probably hidden, or barking too much. There was not enough food, and what there was I did not like. One night Josh put me outside and never called me back or opened the door for me. After a while I decided I would leave and look for another home. I thought it would be easy to find a family who would love me. But I was wrong.

I wonder if Josh ever missed me or if he was relieved. I also wonder what he told Peter? I will never know.

Chapter 5

AFTER I LEFT JOSH I HAD TO LIVE ON THE STREET. I COULD NOT find a new home. This was a very bad experience. I seldom found enough food and what I found was of poor quality since most of it came from garbage pails. Sometimes I was worried that I would get ill. Apparently I have a very strong stomach as nothing happened, except that I was hungry most of the time. Nobody brushed me, so my coat started to look mangy. Nobody talked to me except saying something nasty like "Don't you dare ever to come back." Some people tried to hit me or threw stones after me. No one tried to pet me or hug me; I was very lonely and unhappy.

Nevertheless I did not want to return to Josh. I kept hoping that Peter would come and look for me and find me. I was lucky that it was summer so I was not freezing at night without a warm blanket. Even without enough food I was getting fatter. Something told me I was going to have babies soon, and that I must find a suitable place to live. One day I saw a lovely barn filled with hay, and a house nearby. This was it!

I spent the night in the barn; it was very cozy, with a drinking trough for cattle nearby. So I was not thirsty, just hungry. I had no choice but to look for the owner and try to explain. It did not take him long to understand that I was going to have pups very soon. He did not seem to be overjoyed, but he told me I could stay in the barn, if I was not going to chase any of his animals. He had a lot. Chickens, cows, dogs, horses, even a cat, which I always chase, but I didn't. Thank heavens he had no ducks. I am not sure what I would have done if he had had any.

The farmer had a wife and three children, who were told to stay away from me. He said nothing about food. He should have guessed that I was very hungry. His smallest daughter, Amy, took pity on me, and smuggled some leftovers to me. I licked her hand and made a big fuss about her, so she would continue to do so. Being nice to humans often works. Maybe some humans are not treated nicely by other humans, so they hope to be loved by dogs.

A very nasty hired man lived on the place. He really disliked me. Without any reason, he would hit me or kick me whenever we met. He chased me with sticks and even tried to run over me with his motorcycle. I certainly could not bite him, which I was dying to do, as that would have meant losing my chance to stay in the barn. I tried to keep out of his way, not always successfully. He wore big boots. I have had a horror of big boots and noisy motorcycles ever since. I am still afraid I will be hit.

When the big night arrived, I was ready for my babies. One by one, each little squirming pup descended from my belly. Just like my Mummy told me she had done, I cleaned each pup, arranged them in the hay and taught them how to suck. There were five in all, two girls and three boys. They were beautiful, although a little different looking than me, as their father must have been that collie, not a Chessie. They were very loving. All I could have asked for. Just the timing was so bad. It would have been great to become a mother at Trinity Hall, not in a strange nameless barn without a human or any friend around. No one to admire my babies.

I was very proud of my pups, to me the most beautiful I had ever seen. They all learned to suck without any trouble. However I had the great problem of how to feed myself so I would have enough milk. They seemed hungry all the time. They did nothing but eat, sleep and whimper, probably to get my attention. I licked them and I loved them and told them stories, the same my Mummy had told us. I told them all I could remember. And I made up a few new ones. Small pups do not mind what they hear as long as they know they are loved. Big dogs want to be loved also, especially I.

Soon the pups started to roam around the barn, and I got worried that they might escape and get into trouble. I realized that I must find a permanent home and a new human family as soon as possible before a disaster occurred. One day I was on another trip to find this home and more food, since the scraps Amy gave me were not enough. As usual I was trotting along a road when something too horrible happened to me. A pickup truck stopped next to me. The driver got out and, before I realized what was going on, I found myself inside a large sack with some air holes cut into it. In a split second the sack was fastened on all sides so I could not get out. The sack with me in it got lifted onto the truck where there were already other sacks with dogs inside. We all barked and tried to get out. There was no way. The truck drove off.

When the truck stopped, I was put in a cage just like any other lost dog. A terrible thing had happened to me. I had been taken away from the street to a dog shelter, which seemed like a prison to me. I had lost my collar with my name and address at Trinity Hall, so I could not explain who I really was, that I was not an ordinary stray dog at all. Dogs are not allowed to roam the streets, fend for themselves and live without human parents. Sometimes they get sick or they freeze to death, especially in winter, or they cannot find either water or food. Strange people hit them and mistreat them.

One purpose of an animal shelter is to shelter animals from such dangers. Another purpose is to serve as a place where animals can find people to adopt them—even animals who have been mistreated by cruel humans or had to live on the streets. There is so much unfairness. Everybody seems to be frightened of a mangy-looking, lonely, frightened dog. For a big hunting dog like myself to be put into a cage with nowhere to run was awful. What did the people in the shelter expect from me? Did they expect me to be happy when I could walk only for ten minutes three times a day? I never got a treat. I was never petted or loved. I cried, I howled, I made a lot of noise.

Once in a while a young girl appeared and took some of the dogs, including me, for special walks. Although I was acquiring a very bad reputation, she did not seem to mind. She was called Theresa. I liked that name and I liked her. She brought me some cookies and even a toy bone, so I would have something to occupy myself. Theresa came after school and on weekends. Humans seem to spend a lot of time in schools. I think animal shelters should have lots of helpers. Dogs need more exercise and more loving—especially loving. Without human companionship, they can get very sad, as I did.

I will never forget the time I had to spend in the cage, even when it gave me time to think a lot about life. But it made me a much worse dog. I used to be obedient. I did what I was told. I walked beautifully on a leash, I stayed when I was supposed to stay, I guarded, I came when called. Now I did nothing. I had lost all my manners.

What had happened to my puppies? Whenever I thought about them, I started to cry. Would I ever find them again? The people at the shelter must have seen by the size of my tits that I had had babies. Either they did not care, or they did not know where to find them. I hope that my babies all found as good a home as I have now.

Chapter 6

I WONDERED WHAT HAD HAPPENED TO PETER. HAD HE GOTTEN another dog? Was he upset when he learned that Josh and I could not get along? Did Josh say that it was all my fault? It was not. It was really Josh's fault.

Did Peter search for me? I'm not sure if he did. Certainly the first thing for him to do would have been to contact or to visit shelters. There was only one purebred Chesapeake Bay Retriever at my shelter—me. If Peter had described me, they would have told him right away that I was there. Maybe he called before I arrived, or the shelter people mislaid his telephone number and could not call him back after I came. *He* had to find *me*, as *I* could not find *him*. I did not know the name of the office where he was working. I could not put an ad in the paper. What would I have said?

"Chesapeake Bay Retriever lost her master Peter?" There must be many men called Peter. I did not know where he had gone. I knew exactly where we lived at college, but no one was there during vacation. Now, even when I can run in the country I stay very close to home, because I never want to be lost again. Never!

I tried to run away from the shelter, but I did not succeed. Many people passed my cage, but no one wanted to adopt me. Sometimes I tried very hard to get their attention. The shelter people called me "Brownie!" "Brownie!" What an awful name! I did not come when they called me Brownie. I showed myself from my worst side. I was barking and I would not come close and I would not heel or sit. After a while, the keeper put a large "X" on my cage.

The very next day two ladies stopped at my cage. They were not particularly young, one was dark and one was blond. They jabbered along, asking all kinds of questions about me. Did I know how to walk on a leash? Of course I knew how to walk on a leash, but I was not going to do so. What was my name? Was I housebroken? Then all of a sudden, the dark woman turned away. She said she wanted a small dog. I was "too big and unmannerly." That was not very encouraging.

But after awhile she came back. She decided to take me anyhow. She wanted me to go in her car. After my last experience I mistrusted all strange cars. Two men who worked at the shelter had to lift me in the car. There I was. The lady said to me, "We are going to live together, so you better be nice to me." I grunted. That meant that I was not going to be nice. She seemed unaware of my bad temper.

I should have been grateful that I could leave the shelter, that I'd found a new home—even with my terrible behavior. Much later my new Mom told me that the big black "X" on my cage was a death sentence. She could not bear the thought that I would have to die if she had not taken me. So, against her better judgment, she took me. She had wanted a small, well-behaved dog, certainly not a badly-behaved large hunter.

At least I was not in a cage. Her car with a sunroof was certainly better. I knew that every car ride had to end somewhere. During our ride, the two women questioned whether I had had shots, since the shelter had not given me any. Could they be so stupid to think that I, Kara, would not have had all my shots? I had no way to prove I had. If only I had not lost my collar and tags. If only I had not lost what humans call "my identity."

We stopped at a building where a man in a white coat came out, gave one look at me and said, "Very unfriendly." I was very unfriendly. "I am not going to give her any shots." The lady with the dark hair seemed to be more courageous. She said, "So I will." She went inside the building and came out with a syringe, looked at me and said, "Listen my friend." "My friend?" I wasn't her friend! She went on, "You are going to lie still and you are not going to bite me. I am going to give you some shots and then we are going to your new home." I did not like her, but I never bit her. Now I love her even more than I did my first Mother.

She gave me the shots. She did not even try to pet me. She knew better. But she did give me a cookie. A big bone cookie I like best. She gave me some water and we drove on. It did not take very long. It was a pretty drive. There were other dogs on the road and I could bark at them and at the bicyclists. We passed a motorcycle and I barked even more. I really hate motorcyclists. The terrible man on the farm had had one. I have never forgotten how he mistreated me.

Chapter 7

FINALLY WE STOPPED IN FRONT OF "OUR HOUSE." THE DARK-haired woman opened the door and said, "Here you are." She had decided during the drive that I wasn't going to be called "Brownie." We certainly were in agreement about that! I was going to be called "Dara." Now "Dara" is very close to "Kara," so I liked it. I learned this name immediately. She talked to me and said "Dara, here we are. I want you to be nice to me."

Was I going to be nice to her? No, I was not. But I was not going to be really nasty either. We entered the house, quite a pretty house with a very inviting sofa and a big bowl of food and lots of water. She said, "Eat as much as you can, drink as much as you can and take a rest." Where would I take a rest but on the sofa! Apparently that was her sofa. So we had an argument right away. (Maybe Peter would still find me.)

I made a concession and let her sit on the sofa and I sat on the floor on a nice thick carpet. We looked at each other. She said, "Dara, you are quite pretty! But I thought Chesapeake Retrievers had lots of curls and straight legs. You have neither. You are a strange Chessie." Of course she did not know that I had lost all my curls from my meager diet. And who would have straight legs after living in a cage without being able to run around? Soon I would show her how beautiful I really was.

After a little rest, she and her friend had lunch. I had already had a good meal. She said, "Now, I want you to remember you are called Dara. When we go out and I call you, you have to come, because there are cars around and it is dangerous. You could be run over." She had forgotten that I had lived on the streets and knew quite a lot about cars. She said, "I have a treat for you. You are a Chesapeake Bay Retriever, so you like to swim. We are going to go swimming. We live near a lake. Maybe you will like our lake."

We walked to a little house where she put on a bathing suit. It was a pleasant place to get into the water. I could plunge around and wade. I love to wade. That's what you do when you look for ducks. Then she started to swim. She did not swim like a young Chessie, but she tried her best. I thought I would please her and swim with her. We swam across the lake. I could have gone twice across the lake in the time it took her to do it once, but I slowed down and swam in circles. On the other side of the lake I could roam around freely in the garden of one of her friends. I heard her call me. It was time to swim back. She was very pleased with me because I came when she called me and I swam so well.

She decided that I had to lie down and wait until she read the newspaper. Obviously I wanted to inspect all the surroundings and sniff them and see where I was. So I took off. That made her very mad. She came after me with a leash and said that would never do. "When I say 'stay,' that means stay. And when I say we are going for a walk, we are going for a walk."

I was not allowed to inspect the countryside by myself. Another concession. So she tied me up until she was ready, not when I was ready, to go home. She did not understand that I was curious about this new place. However, she let me sniff at everything whilst I walked with her. She showed me a big flower bed and said, "Dara, you are not allowed to lie on the flowers. You can sniff them, you can look at them, but you cannot lie on them." I have never seen anybody having so many flowers. All colors, all smells, very pretty. We walked all over the place. It was a little village, totally different to what I was used to.

That night, when it was time to go to bed, my new mother said, "If you want to come into my room and lie on the carpet and not disturb me, you can do so. Otherwise, you will stay alone in the living room." That seemed preferable to me, because I thought finally I could sleep on the sofa. But she arranged the pillows in such a way that I could not. So maybe it was better to go to bed with her. She had a huge bed. "No" again. She told me I was too big and my nails too long to sleep with her in her bed. Against my will, I decided to do as I was told and I stayed on the floor without arguing.

The next day, she took me out in the car. I sat in the back and started to bark as loud as I could. She hated that. "Don't bark!" I continued. Finally, in a very stern voice, "If you continue to bark, we will go home and I will drive alone." We made another compromise. I barked a little, she was only a little angry. This drive ended in a walk. She was not going to take me on the leash. I was supposed to stay with her. A new decision. Would I run away? No. I decided to stay close.

Later that day, I heard a young woman, her daughter, call her "Mom," so I decided to call her Mom, as well. She could not be called Mother. That was for Mother at Trinity Hall, but "Mom" seemed all right.

That afternoon, Mom and I went swimming again. We had a lovely afternoon in the water. She had two tennis balls with her and I showed her how well I could retrieve two balls at a time. She was amazed. At the end I was not going to give them to her. So she used a third one. I could not take three balls in my mouth without dropping one. We started to play all over again.

By the time we went home, it was time for my dinner. I was very hungry. I was not used to so much exercise anymore, but I felt much better. I allowed her to pet me once, just once. She did not try anymore.

Mom tried very hard to like me. I must admit that I did not make it easy for her. I was nasty to everybody who came to my house. So many people came into my garden, onto my beach, onto my tennis court, in my car. I had so many things I was supposed to share and guard. I did not like that. However, I liked to steal sandwiches from strangers at the lake. Quite unnecessary. I got more than enough to eat at home. It was just fun. Mom was telling me all the time that I had to try to behave or we could not live together. Mom never hit me, even when I was very naughty. Whenever she gets really unhappy with me, she says, "Dara, Dara, how can you do that? How can you do that to me?"

I had gotten so provoked by the horrible life on the street and in the cage and losing my pups that I had become very aggressive. When people came to visit, I had no intention of letting them in. I showed my big teeth and barked very loudly. However, these strangers were let in and I was locked up until the strangers, who seemed to be friends of Mom, had entered. Then I was expected to behave, lie down and be quiet.

I did nothing, and I mean nothing, that I was supposed to do. I knew perfectly well how to walk on a leash. I knew the meaning of "lie" and "stay." I just would not do most things Mom asked me to do. When Mom wanted to stroke me, I thought at first she was going to hit me. Of course she would not. I feel bad, and quite ashamed of all the difficulties I caused Mom and still cause her sometimes.

Once, on a snowy day, she wore big boots. I got so excited that I nearly bit her, until she explained that the boots were to keep her feet dry and had nothing to do with me. I, of course, immediately thought of that brutal farmhand. Some bad memories I cannot forget. This accounts for my acting so nasty to strangers. I never know if I can trust them. Of course the more I show my teeth, the more frightened and angry they become.

I hope Mom has forgiven me and will always do so. When I ask her, she tells me that she has. Now she always whispers to me that she loves me. She tries to see only my good sides and to forget my bad ones. Looking back on those first weeks, I realize that Mom must have been an angel to keep me. I do not believe that anybody else would have put up with me.

After I had been at her house for a while, a young man called Andrew came to stay with us. He was quite wonderful. He was the first person whom I allowed to pet me and stroke me as much as he liked. A new Peter? He almost changed my terrible disposition back to my former self.

Andrew was, and is, a very special person in my life. He knew everything I liked to do. He loved to run with me, to play ball, to stroke my belly, to tell me all kinds of stories. Later, whenever he came back from college he visited me. Sometimes he spent the night in our guest room. That was the best. The guest room has two beds next to each other. Most nights I managed to get in his room and, after he was asleep, jump on the second bed, which was strictly forbidden by Mom, but of course she did not know. In the middle of the night I would get closer and closer to Andrew, until he started to stroke me in his sleep. A wonderful sensation. Sometimes he got tired of me and threw me out. You cannot be lucky all the time. Through Andrew I learned how important it is to have good friends.

After a few weeks Mom decided that I had to drive with Andrew to her winter house. No more country life. I had again a very long trip with Andrew, about the same kind of trip I had had with Peter: long, long highways with booths manned by people in uniform. I barked like crazy, as I hate people in uniforms. Andrew was considerate and stopped often to let me out to drink and eat and walk a little. He played music and talked to me. Finally we stopped at a large house. It was in a "suburb," just outside a city. Definitely not Trinity Hall, but it was bigger than our house in the country.

Chapter 8

So there we were. Andrew and I in a new house, but no Mom. Where was she? Was she going to come? She had told me she was going to come. It took her another day. I am not sure how she got here. Finally, she arrived. I was so happy to see her, and she seemed happy to see me.

The house had lots of sofas. They were all very inviting. But Mom definitely told me that I was not to lie on them. She would get very angry if I did. However, sometimes I managed a little snooze on one or the other. We made a compromise. There was a sofa upstairs which she did not like as much, although she used it during the day. She allowed me to sleep on it. She would give me my own sheet at night so I would know it was mine.

What a totally different life in Mom's winter house. Mom had less time for me, mostly only on weekends. She was busy working at her desk in her office, or going out to her studio—she is an artist—or playing tennis. I could come along to her studio where I could watch her work. It did not seem very interesting to me, but at least we were together. In the garden was another tennis court which took up a lot of room. I do not know why Mom was so crazy about tennis. I would have preferred a pool, but there was none, not even a fishpond, which is enough to get cool. Thank heavens the neighbors had one.

Later I found out that Mom had a lot of friends with swimming pools, where she went often. Sometimes she took me along and sometimes I had to stay at home, where I sulked. Probably some of her friends did not like me. In the beginning I was nasty to everyone I did not know. Even to some I knew, but did not like. Not all humans like all dogs, but all dogs are supposed to like all humans. Some dogs wiggle their tails at everybody they meet. I feel that that is a lack of character.

Just like in the country, too many people were constantly coming to my house. This was my new house, which I now had to guard by barking at everyone and showing my teeth to prevent them from coming in. Mom informed me that she appreciated it if I barked to announce somebody, but that was enough. One bark, maybe two, then I was supposed to sit down and be friendly, just like in the country. Well, I wasn't. We had another quarrel. To make up, I told Mom that I liked her and that she could stroke me as much as she wanted. As a matter of fact, she never stroked me enough. I loved to have my stomach tickled at all times, day and night. And I loved her to tickle me behind my ears. She was obliging to do so. She never forgot to kiss me goodnight. A real kiss. No one had ever done that before. And I gave her a kiss. She went to her room and I went on my sofa and then we went to sleep. Sometimes she visited me in the middle of the night, probably to see whether I was comfortable or maybe she was lonely for me. We talked a little and we snuggled a little and then everybody went back to sleep.

Humans have so many strange ideas. Mom certainly had plenty of them. I had to go to a new veterinarian. More injections. She left me at the doctor's and went home alone. How could that be? I was not going to stay at the vet's! A strong young man came and, believe it or not, put me into a cage. Was I going to be locked up again? This time in a place run by a vet? What was wrong with Mom? The same man came back and poked me with a needle and I went to sleep.

I can't tell you what happened. I can't remember anything except when I woke up I was very drowsy and I had a pain in my tummy. They gave me another injection and I went back to sleep. They probably realized that I had a lot of pain. The next day Mom came back. I was still quite sleepy and not feeling too well. She and the young man put me into the car and she took me home. Now, what on earth was all this about?

Mom told me that I would never have babies again. She explained to me that there were too many dogs in the world, that many dogs must be prevented from getting puppies, except when they live with humans who want to have more dogs. Many humans only want pure-breds; maybe that is why so many mixed-breed dogs live on the street. I was one exception. Even my puppies might have been odd looking when they got bigger although they were adorable when I last saw them.

After a few days I had to go back to the vet. I didn't want to, but Mom promised that she would stay with me. He took out some stitches and said that I was healing very well and that I was going to be fine in a few days. I was not to run around as much as usual. So I stayed at home and in a few days I felt just like before.

Chapter 9

I OFTEN WENT OUT ON THE STREET ALONE, WHICH I WAS NOT supposed to do. So one day Mom ordered an electric fence around the whole garden and put a special collar on me. I couldn't get out without getting a shock every time I tried to leave. Who wants to get an electric shock? Even when something very interesting happened outside on the street, it seemed wiser not to try. The garden had big hedges for me to jump over; this I liked very much, since it reminded me of the jumps with Karim and Filou.

I began to make dog friends in the neighborhood. One was named Lance, and he came to play with me every day for a while until he moved away.

I made another friend, the most unlikely friend you could imagine. Mom was often invited to visit friends who had a big house and a swimming pool that I was allowed to use. So of course the first thing I did when I arrived there was to swim. These friends also had the funniest dog—tiny, and very playful. He only reached to my ankles. We got along very well. It was as though I had found my puppies again, as he was only a puppy when we met. I was so much bigger that I could take him in my mouth. and carry him around. His mother thought I was going to crush him. Of course I did not. I taught him a lot: how to run, how to swim, how to get in and out of the pool and how to play with a tennis ball. He was not very good at first, but he learned quickly.

Like all pups he grew bigger and bigger, but not very big, just half my size. We invented our own games, rather rough games. He was a sturdy dog. He liked rough games. We barked and barked, at least that is what the humans thought. We really talked about a lot of things they couldn't understand. For them it was just barking. "Quiet, don't bark. We are going to play tennis. We have guests, we are going to have lunch." There was always some reason why we should be nice and quiet, well-behaved dogs, just to be seen and not heard, like some children.

It was a marvelous way to spend a day or an afternoon. In and out of the pool, someone to play with, to run with and to talk to. We are still friends, but he no longer lives in his big house. I do not see him often anymore as he now lives in France and comes seldom to the U.S. He has never visited me in the country although I have invited him. I do not like his mother very much. I liked his dad a lot.

Many people came to my house during that fall. They all told Mom that I was a very difficult dog, "Why did she want to live with me? I was beautiful, but difficult, totally unsuitable for her and for a house near a city. I was a hunting dog, and should live in the country. Why didn't she give me to someone in the country?" Still Mom was too kind for that. She knew I would be miserable to change homes again. We had gotten used to each other. At least I had gotten used to her. I had started even to love her.

I am not sure whether she had gotten used to me. I would not sit, I would not stay, I ate up my car, took big chunks out of it. It looked like hell. When she was totally frustrated with me, she asked me "Dara, why do you do this to me?" When I was taken for a walk, I was chasing cars, chasing bicycles, chasing cats. I did everything to make myself really unpopular. So Mom decided to put me in a boarding school to learn how to behave again.

I really wanted to live with Mom, but I did not want to go to boarding school. She didn't ask me. She just took me to the country where a nasty-looking man came out of his house, took a leash, took me away and told me that in 10 days I would be a new dog. I did not want to be a new dog. I wanted to be just like I was. Mom left. She told me that she would come back at the end of 10 days. But did she mean it?

Or was she tired of me and had gotten rid of me? What a terrible thought. She did not kiss me good-bye.

I heard a lot of dogs barking. but I was not allowed to play with them. I was not put in a cage, but it was something like it. I could run around a bit, but not very much and I was never allowed to run outside, although there was a big outside.

Always on a leash, always being told just what to do: "Heel, sit, heel, do not pull, stay, sit, heel." What kind of conversation was that? Nobody ever talked pleasantly to me or told me that I was beautiful or nice. Just five words: heel, sit, slow, stay, come. And sometimes, very rarely, if I did everything I was supposed to do the man said, "Good girl." Nobody petted me. Nobody kissed me. It really was miserable.

After 10 days, Mom came back as she had promised. She did keep her word. This man told her that I now had really good manners. He was going to show Mom just how well I walked on the leash, sit, heel, stay. I did everything exactly right. The man was too nasty when I didn't do what he wanted me to do. Mom was very impressed.

We got back in my car. Again, I just could not resist taking another big bite out of the seat. So Mom said, "You certainly haven't forgotten how to tear up the car. I wonder if you learned how to walk with me."

We arrived back home and had a little snuggling session. Then Mom told me that I was going to do all the commands for her, as I had done for that unpleasant man. Unfortunately, I did not. I should have pleased her. But she had left me for so long, I had to get even. It was not the right thing to do.

For a while I walked on the street quite like a lady, but then I saw a squirrel. I forgot everything. I pulled and I pulled and Mom could not hold me and I ran after the squirrel. The squirrel was much faster than I. I have never caught one yet. When I came back, I tried to apologize and I heeled for a little while. I still was pretty bad with Mom and I still disappointed her.

I did not stay every time she asked me to. I was not nice to visitors most of the time. I just do not like to be left out of anything, not even Mom's conversation with her friends. I like to be the center of her attention. I know this is not possible. Sometimes I am polite and sit and watch without stealing food or making a nuisance of myself, like insisting that Mom play with me, either with my ball or my toys. If she does not, I bark—a lot. I can tell when Mom gets really fed up. That's when I stop.

Chapter 10

LIFE WENT ALONG QUITE PLEASANTLY WITHOUT GREAT EXCITE-ment, only Mom went away too often, sometimes for hours, sometimes for days. I was left alone with Maria, the housekeeper, and Matthew, who had moved to my house. I think he only moved because he wanted to be with me. We had long talks at night. He did not go out as much as Mom. We were at home together. We went to the studio, as he was also an artist and liked to go there to paint. He did different things than Mom.

Just like her, he seemed to love being in the studio. He also did not care if it was day or night. Whenever he had time he took me for walks and we played with tennis balls. I nearly fell in love with him. He was very much like Peter, and Andrew—a dreamer. He was not pushy, he was not insisting, really very pleasant. He loved going for walks in the park and along the canal. He was so nice that I would oblige him and not attack cyclists. After all, they should have their fun, too. I would mind my own business.

Only when I saw ducks, that was another matter. When I saw a duck, I had to swim after it and chase it, much more exciting than squirrels. As I told you, I was a very fast swimmer, but I had lost my timing. I never caught a duck and I could never persuade one to swim where I wanted it to. When they had enough of me, they just flew into the air. Since nobody shot them, they just flew away and came down farther up the canal. I had trouble getting there before they flew away again. I believe they didn't like the game of tag very much. I couldn't understand what they said to each other, but there was a lot of very excited quacking. Maybe they said "let's wait for the dog" and maybe they said "let's not." The upshot was they did sometimes and sometimes they didn't. Chasing ducks was the highlight of our walks.

I was supposed to be on a leash on the path along the canal, but usually I ran free, except when I attacked the cyclists. I learned quickly that this wasn't to my advantage, since I had to go back on the leash for a while. You can't always have your own way. After all, chasing cyclists is not as much fun as chasing ducks.

I am not sure why humans want to change things when life is pleasant. They get another idea and want to do something totally different. One day, Matthew decided he wanted to move away. He wanted to live with a human girl. He told me that he loved me very much but that he loved the girl more. How stupid! He didn't understand that he would have lots of trouble, whereas I gave him no trouble whatsoever!

He continued to come once or twice a week to take me for a walk. I believe he walked with me because he felt lonely for me or maybe he felt bad towards Mom, because he had promised her to help her look after me. The other days I had to go for walks with our housekeeper Maria, who walked so slowly you can't imagine. Mom usually only walked on the weekends. That was the best. Some days she walked early in the morning or at night when she came home.

By now Mom and I had lived together for quite a while. We were both getting older. Quite honestly, it seemed to me that it was more noticeable with Mom than with me. After her shoulder operations she no longer played tennis, which suited me very well as I did not like her tennis friends. Most of them made a nasty fuss when I was there.

I did not see how I disturbed them. I only kept the balls they hit out of the court onto the grass, and I sometimes growled at one or the other if I did not like them. I never bit anyone, although some of them pretended that I had done so. Humans can be so tiresome.

One pretty young woman named Lisa had played ladies doubles on a very hot day. After tennis she invited Mom and me for a swim in her pool. A lovely idea. I was very pleased. It was a big pool. Mom and I were swimming together, whilst

Lisa disappeared in the house. She was getting us something to drink. When she came back towards Mom with a tray, it seemed menacing to me, as I was not sure what it meant. Obviously I started to growl at her and show my teeth, which I always do as a precaution. Lisa got frightened and upset and informed me she would never invite me again. She never did.

Mom has two children, a daughter, Martha, and a son, Louis. Mom told me that her daughter lived in Europe and mostly came to visit in the country, which she likes better than the city, just like me. Apart from that, we didn't have much in common. Contrary to Mom, she was not crazy about dogs and could not see my good sides. We just tolerated each other. Louis lives near us in the country in a lovely place, but he owns two dogs and two cats, so I can't visit him, and he does not take much notice of me when he visits Mom. I believe he likes animals a lot, just not me. I am not sure why. Is he jealous?

Chapter 11

LAST SUMMER, WHEN WE WERE IN THE COUNTRY, MOM TOLD ME that Maria, her housekeeper and friend for 25 years had suddenly died. By now I knew that "dead" meant you will never see each other again. What will I do without Maria, who had become my companion when Mom was not around? Who will feed me and play with me? I loved her even if she walked too slowly and I loved it when she called me "la loca," which means "crazy one." She did not really mean it. She taught me Spanish. I can understand three languages, since Mom often talks to me in German. Three languages is quite a lot for a Chessie, especially since I do not mix them up.

Mom went back to our winter home near the city for a few days and got even more interested in what she calls "the cemetery." This is a large grassy place, where it is fun to run around and play in between all kinds of stones. Some looked like the stone where Mother is. Mom always went to the same place, the only one with flowers, but it is not as beautiful as her garden.

One day more flowers and a new stone arrived. Mom told me that it was in honor of Maria, who had wanted to be close to the family. Mom's husband is under one stone, he is also dead. Mom told me that she had chosen a very large white stone for herself. But she is not dead, thank heavens. She must never go under that stone. I will always guard her. Always!

Mom likes to talk about Rottweilers. I find them very ugly. Dogs without tails look most peculiar. They have to wiggle half their bodies to show that they are happy. Mom lived with a Rottweiler before she met me. The Rottweiler died, but she was very old. Mom apparently liked her very much, although she assures me not as much as me. As I told you, Mom does not always tell the truth, if she thinks it makes me sad. So I am not sure. There is a little park for that Rottweiler, opposite the tennis court in the country; it has a stone with her name and lots of flowers. Apparently, unlike me, she loved to watch tennis when Mom played.

I have simple tastes. I like to eat, to swim, to go for walks at least twice a day, to be petted a lot, to sleep on beds or sofas, to drive in a car, especially to fly in a plane, and to be included in everything Mom is doing. I hate to stay alone at home. I told this so often to Mom. We just cannot agree all the time when it is my turn to come along, or when I have to stay and guard our house.

Humans do not seem to realize that protecting Mom is my most important duty. I do it at times when it is not appropriate, this is certain. There are many decisions which I have to make very quickly. At times I do something without thinking.

Most of the workmen who come to the house to fix something call Mom first to ask that I be locked up. They do not understand that I do not want anyone to enter the house without me inspecting them very carefully. This means loud barks, showing my teeth, not biting, mind you, but my teeth are large and menacing, and a lot of sniffing. Some repairmen get so scared they leave before they finish their job.

Mom explained to me over and over that I was a watchdog, and have to guard the house when I am alone. However, if a human was around, I only was supposed to bark once or twice, and then let the human decide if they wanted to open the door or not. Once the door was opened, I was supposed to be quiet and polite. This is very difficult for me because I get easily excited when strangers are around. Sometimes I get locked up as a punishment or for the peace of mind of the visitor.

I always think it is better to be on the safe side, so I just bark and bark until Mom comes and checks. I recognize the people who come often, like the gardener, the handyman and the plumber, who seem to be here all the time, and I know most of Mom's friends. Some I like, others complain that I bark too much or say that they are afraid to come in the house: "I will not come near the house. I am sure Dara will bite me." They should know by now that I only show my teeth. I do not bite!

I do not like to be left at home alone at night. It is never a whole night; it is really just the evening because Mom always comes back rather early. She gets picked up by a man or a woman. That I do not like at all. I am supposed to be polite when somebody comes to fetch her. I know they have come to take Mom away because she is dressed up and smells of perfume. When they leave, I go to my sofa and sulk. Sometimes I will not greet Mom when she returns. I do not even come downstairs, just to show her that my feelings were hurt.

Mom gets impatient with me when I do not understand what she wants me to do. Most of the time I understand, but I do not always want to do it. She expects me to be good all the time. To really irritate me she tells me how good that Rottweiler was, that she always did what she was told, that she was never a nuisance, and that nobody was frightened of her except bad guys, not friends. Mom can go on and on. It is lucky I never met that dog. I am certain I would not have liked her.

Chapter 12

L IFE HAD GOTTEN SOME KIND OF ROUTINE, IF ANYONE COULD
call Mom's schedule a routine. We spent two months of
the summer in the country and two weeks around Christmas in the winter, as well as some occasional weekends.
Every time our stay passes much too rapidly. I prefer the life
and the house in the country to the life in town. Mom is
more relaxed and spends more time with me. It is also
where she found me. She never asked me how old I was but
decided that my birthday was August 13, the day we met. I
always get a steak slightly broiled how I like it best.

Mom has a talent for making me feel very important. I
expect she does that also to humans as she has so many
friends, but no husband. She told me that she is a widow,
and that there is no man in the house, so I have to look after

her. This is fine with me. I do not like men very much, only a few like Andrew, Matthew and the gardener.

I have my own lawyer. Everybody seems to need a lawyer. Mine is called Dan and is very helpful. It seems a little strange that a dog needs a lawyer, but I really do and did. He set up the foundation for my book royalties and he helped Mom with my lawsuit. This is what happened: Mom has this very unpleasant neighbor, who owns a nasty little dog. I get along well with all dogs unless they try to provoke me. This woman and her dog have the terrible habit of standing in front of my driveway and the dog never stops yapping. One time, I ignored the shock from the electric fence and ran on the street to tell the dog to shut up and to go away. I showed my teeth to the neighbor, which frightened her so much that she fell over backwards.

Even though her doctor found nothing wrong with her and the vet found nothing wrong with her dog, she filed a complaint against me. Mom had to appear in the animal court with our lawyer. Six witnesses appeared with the woman. They were all neighbors, and every one said something nasty about me. I do not know how this was possible! One said I was trained as an attack dog. Ridiculous! Mom instructs me all the time to be nice and kind, especially to our neighbors.

The judge decided I would always have to walk on a leash or Mom would be fined. Mom had already reinforced the current in the electric fence and moved it closer to the house. I cannot get to the street, even in emergencies. The woman got her day in court and I got trapped inside the fence!

The neighbors didn't care that I once saved Mom, something that she has never forgotten. On one of our walks in the neighborhood, we came to a street that had been newly tarred. Since there were no longer barricades, Mom thought the tar was dry. Suddenly, one of her shoes got stuck and she fell forward on the street and could not get up. I got very frightened and looked for help. I could not see anyone, so I went into the middle of the street, sat down and barked and barked. I kept hoping a car would come and slow down but not run over me. In a few minutes, a car did just that. The lady driving stopped, saw Mom lying there and got out to see what had happened. Women do not usually lie face-down in the street. By this time, Mom could move and the lady helped her get up. Mom was limping badly so the lady insisted on driving us home, me included. Neither the lady nor Mom could get over how clever I had been summoning help. I love Mom more than my safety.

I must try to be nicer to the neighbors. I would rather be loved than disliked. If you have once created a bad image, it is most difficult to change that. Some of Mom's friends still are frightened of me, which makes me sad. Others are happy when I am around. I only sniff everyone very carefully. Mom put up signs that say "Please do NOT touch the dog." I get nervous when a stranger tries to stroke me. I am still afraid that I might get hit, as I was when I lived on the street and on the farm. Bad memories from long ago.

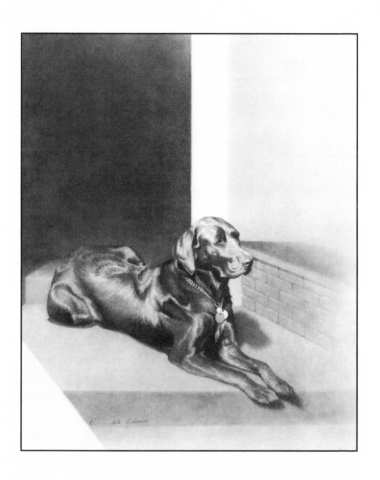

Chapter 13

W E SPENT LAST CHRISTMAS IN THE COUNTRY, AS USUAL, WITH both of Mom's children and a grandchild, plus assorted nieces and make-believe grandchildren. It was glorious. Mom could not ski anymore, not even cross-country, which I love, but we walked together. She hoped I understood that she could not do as much with me as before. I really tried, but who wants to be a sedentary hunting dog? All our guests took turns taking me for long walks. Some walked as fast as Mom used to. That was great, but I always missed her. Sometimes I also have pains when walking, but I can still run and jump over hedges. I also have to rest more. Growing older seems to bring pains and illness. I now have a white beard which I want to have dyed. Mom said "no," although she dyes her own hair, I know. I also have arthritis and a slightly displaced hip.

A new year started, Mom told me. We celebrated New Year's Eve together with some of her friends and family. I got a very special bone. They all drank champagne, but nobody offered me any. I am not sure that I would like champagne. Everybody made New Year's resolutions. So I made a couple myself. Can I stick to them?

Resolution one: I will not chase cats. Sometimes I mistake cats for squirrels. Mom does not mind when I chase squirrels except when I am on the leash and pull her. I will not bite a cat. When a cat stands still I stand still and look at it. When it runs again, I run after it until it stands still again. Some cats are stupid and forget to climb a tree. Cats get very frightened by my barking and my teeth.

Resolution two: I will not chase squirrels when I am on the leash with Mom. I am very good until I see a squirrel. I just have to run after it. I know that Mom cannot hold me when I do that, because I am very strong and she is not. Only Andrew or Matthew can hold me. This resolution is also hard to keep. Squirrels are clever, they always run up a tree. I've never caught a squirrel yet. I nearly caught one once, because it had been hit by a car and couldn't climb very well. That was not a real chase. I can't climb a tree, although I often try.

When Mom and I go for a walk, she always lets me run loose. I come back right away when she calls me. I am very careful when I cross the street, I remember that cars are dangerous. I look where they are, and I do not run in front of them, even when something tempting is on the other side of the street. I do not want to be run over. I do not even want to be touched by a car. Once a car sideswiped me just a little. That was very unpleasant. I was limping for days. The driver of the car felt very bad and stopped to apologize. But I don't think it was all his fault. It really did not hurt me too much; I limped more than I had to just to get Mom's sympathy.

The older I get, the more philosophical I become, and the more I appreciate my belongings. I have two houses and a car. I get reprimanded when I tear the seats. Maybe, if the car gets another new seat, I will be more careful. I still wish Mom had a plane. It would be nicer if Mom would never travel or if I could go everywhere with her. Mom sees to it that I am well looked after when she is away. I am never left alone.

Mom told me recently that she thinks I need a dog companion, someone to play with when she is out. I try to tell her firmly that I do not. I only need her, or if Andrew or Matthew came back to live with us, that would be great. I certainly do not need a dog! Then I would get only half of Mom's attention. I hope she forgets that crazy idea. I no longer like to play with dogs. I used to love to play with them, but now I rather like to do my own things.

How can I make Mom understand that I prefer to live in the country? The house there is much more to my liking; my bed is right in the middle of the living room and everybody passing by has to talk to me. Both the inside and the outside are much more satisfying. I would like to go back to the snow. I like to cross-country ski, and I love to walk in the woods and swim in the lake. I also like to go shopping with Mom. Even if nobody likes me in their stores, I love the drives.

Another reason I like living in the country so much is Lucy, who is a lovely golden retriever. She belongs to the store in my village. As soon as we arrive in the country, Lucy tries to move into our house. Many dogs come to visit me in the country because we have such a beautiful place. I have hidden many bones since Mom always brings me new ones. I do not finish them all at once, so I hide them. Lucy did not come just because of those hidden bones. She came to play with me and stay with me. She likes to sit near our new pool, although she never goes in, just like me, because Mom keeps the pool very warm. We swim together in the lake. Lucy loves to ride in the car and to go for walks in the woods. She also likes the smells, and we pretend to hunt together. She realizes that I am dog number one, that the bed is mine, that I have to have more room in the car and that Mom has to pet me first. Lucy is a perfect friend, as she likes to do all the same things as I, but lets me lead in every way. I am not good at being number two. Lucy and I have been friends for many years. She is the one exception to my new feeling of not liking dog companions.

A Summer Day in
the Country

Not Me!!

Where is my breakfast?

Helping in the garden

Opening my car

Picking up the mail with Mom

Retrieving a tennis ball from the pool

Guarding the balls during intermission

Getting ready to swim

Swimming across the lake

Coming home with Mom

Correcting my book

Taking a much needed rest after a strenuous day

Chapter 14

Today I sit at Mom's feet, dictating my story. She often knows what I think, as I know what she thinks, but sometimes we both make mistakes. I like it when Mom uses the computer. She learned it especially to help me write my book. That was very nice of her. I do not believe she is good at it, but she is trying. I cannot use a computer at all.

Our beautiful stay in the country came to an end, like many before, and life in town started again. I can tell when it is Saturday or Sunday, because our secretary, Sally, does not come. It means I have Mom to myself and that she is not so rushed. She takes me for a walk and she takes me shopping, so I get to ride in the car with her. I like to do errands with Mom and wait for her in the car. I will not let anybody come near the car. No one is even allowed to touch it. Mom finds that very practical. She leaves the top open and nobody dares to come close. Nobody dares to come near the house either. I like Sally. She pets me a lot and gives me half her lunch, so I do not have to steal it. However, her presence totally absorbs Mom's attention. When Mom is not around, Sally makes sure that I get my walks and am fed and brushed on time.

Mom has gotten better. She never calls me by the name of that old Rottweiler and has stopped talking to me about her. After all, that dog has been gone a long time, about as long as I am living with Mom. I came just two weeks after her death. I did not even try to replace her. I think I was jealous. I just want to be Dara.

One thing I really hate is when people say, "Hello, Puppy." Everybody can see that I have a white beard, that I am not a puppy. I do not like to be called "dog" either. I am Dara. After all, humans don't like "Hi, human." They have names, and they want them used, just like me.

Humans think the only thing dogs like to do is eat. It is true that I love to eat, especially, something special like chicken or hamburger. I love sauce on my food. I like rice, spaghetti and milk. In fact, I like nearly everything. I love hot sandwiches. I even like cold ones. I do not like tomatoes, salad or raw vegetables. I really like to eat all the food I see, even from the plates of guests. Therefore I do not get invited to Mom's parties anymore.

I adore to go for a walk or for a run. I especially like to go to the park and to the canal and I love to go swimming, just not in warm water. I love to play with balls, especially with someone who can throw them far. I like to retrieve them, but I don't always like to give them up. I like to have a ball in the car, but I do not need one in a plane. I prefer a plane ride to anything else.

Mom was, and still is, amazed at how good I am in a plane, totally different to my behavior in the car. I sit down. never say a word, even if I cannot sit on a seat. I hope that Mom's very generous brother will continue to pay for the plane ride to the country, since Mom is too frugal to pay for one herself. The plane goes so fast. I hate the long car ride and so does Mom.

There are a few other things I do not like. I do not like to be left at home. I do not like to be ignored, even for a little while. I hate going to the vet. And I really do not like the cranky little dog that got me into trouble with the law!

I am trying to teach Mom to understand what I want to do. I am not always successful. She is trying to teach me what she wants me to do to please her. She is also not always successful. I really like to make her happy and I try. To tell the truth, Mom is not perfect either, but she is nearly so.

When Mom travels and comes back, I do everything to please her. First I sulk as I always do, but after a little while I forgive her. We go through that same routine every time. When she has unpacked her suitcases and tidied up, she gives me a present and strokes me and tells me how much she missed me, and I tell her how much I missed her. Of course, she knows it. I always tell her that I am trying to be good and do more things to make her happy. Then she might not go away again.

Chapter 15

MOM LOVES TO GO TO PARTIES, ESPECIALLY IF SHE HAS WORKED all day at her desk, her studio or her office. When she comes home after parties, she tells me if she had a good time or not. I am not sure if she is always quite truthful, as Mom knows so well that I am sad to be left alone and hope she was bored, so maybe she would not go out again.

One evening seemed different. Mom told me she had met someone who lived on the Chesapeake Bay and invited her and me for the following Sunday. This person lived with some Chesapeake Retrievers. I actually had nearly forgotten about the Bay, so many new things had happened in my life. However, when Mom continued to tell me that I had to be really good and not embarrass her, as she was sure I would have a great day, some memories came back to me. I was delighted with the thought of going to the Bay. I might even find an old friend. When would it be Sunday? Maybe I should try not to annoy Mom the next few days, or she might not take me after all.

Sunday came very soon. We had breakfast and I got a special brushing. I looked handsome. Mom was proud of me. I got a ball and off we went in my car. It was a beautiful day with not too many cars on the road. Mom is a good driver. I felt excited and happy, especially that I did not have to stay at home alone. Mom should take me along wherever she goes, but she seldom takes me to parties. After awhile I started to relax and lay down for a bit. Suddenly the countryside seemed to be familiar, as if I had been there before. Mom stopped in front of a beautiful house. This was it, Trinity Hall. I started to shake all over. I think Mom worried that I was ill. I had no time to explain.

Three Chessies were running towards the car making the appropriate noise, half welcoming and half warning. By this time I was out of the car deciding if I should be friendly, as Mom had told me, or aloof. Suddenly the biggest Chessie ran up to me and started kissing and licking me. Could it be Karim? Had I found him again? I started to sniff and to talk to him. No doubt! It was Karim. A little older than when I had seen him last, but just as loving and beautiful. By this time lots of humans came out of the door to greet Mom and, I suppose, to look at me. So I looked at them more closely. Dad was one of them. He also got all startled when he looked at me. "Could it be Kara whom we all thought we had lost forever?" He called "Kara." I interrupted kissing Karim, and came over to him. Mom shouted "Please do not touch Dara," as she had done so often. Dad did not seem to hear. He just repeated over and over "Kara, Kara, you came back after all these years." I licked his hand, just as I had done in the past, and snuggled up to him for a bit.

However I really wanted to get back to Karim. Mom did not understand what was happening. She probably thought that I had gone crazy. Karim wanted to be alone with me, no humans, no other Chessies. So off we went towards our pond, towards the Bay. We took a long swim together, and Karim showed me all the places we used to go to and play. My dream had come true. I met Karim again, and we were together at Trinity Hall. How could I ever leave here? Without any doubt this was the most wonderful moment I had ever experienced.

Finally we decided to return to the house. I was sure Mom was worried by now. I usually stayed very close to her. Dad came to me and stroked me over and over, telling me that he could never part with me again. He invited me to move back to Trinity Hall and restart my former life. Of course Karim wanted me to stay. He did not leave my side for a second.

So what was I going to do? I was dying to stay at the Bay. There was no other place in the world so beautiful. However, I had given my promise to Mom that I would look after her, and that I would never leave her. After all, she had rescued me from a terrible fate, and I realized that I had made her life very difficult. I had a long discussion with Karim and explained to him how much I loved him but that I just could not leave Mom. He understood. I promised, and Mom promised, that we would come back and visit as often as possible, and that Karim would visit me. Maybe he could come one summer to our country house. We would never again be separated for a long time.

Dad invited me to a duck shoot. He hoped that I had not forgotten how to retrieve. I wonder myself. Some things one does not forget. We left after a delicious meal, especially prepared by Cook, including all my favorite things. Cook also wanted me to stay. She believed I would decide via my tummy. The decision had to come from my heart. Mom actually cried a little when I went towards our car, and made it clear to her that I was staying with her because I loved her even more than Karim and the Bay.

Mom was so happy and so touched by my decision that she could hardly drive, as she wanted to stroke me all the time. What an incredible experience this had been, one I can never forget.

Dad and Mom kept their promises. Karim and I get together often. The next time I visited, Peter was there to see me. I tried to ask him how it was possible that he never looked for me after learning I had left his friend Josh. Either he did not care to tell me, or he did not understand my question. We never became close again, as I could not forgive him, whatever his reason. Maybe it was better that he did not tell me. I had dreamed so many dreams about finding Trinity Hall and Karim again. All my dreams ended sadly, but this time life was better than my dreams.

Epilogue
Why did I write this book?

LAST SUMMER, AFTER EIGHT YEARS, MOM AND I AGAIN VISITED the shelter where I stayed in what would have been the last weeks of my life.

It is difficult for me to imagine that humans will part with their most loyal friend—a dog. Many do. Some humans have a good reason, like getting too old or sick or they lose their own home. However, others just abandon their dogs when they get tired of the responsibility. It is nearly impossible for abandoned dogs to find a good new home by themselves. Therefore, a shelter has to help. Shelters have to take care of dogs: help us to get well, since lost dogs are often in terrible condition; feed dogs back to their regular weight; and, most important, give us human warmth and attention so that even difficult dogs can be lucky enough to find a new home. I was a perfect example. All this takes a lot of money and a lot of caring.

Recently, my shelter started a new "Foster Family Adoption Program." It must be hard for a dog to live with a new family for a while and, after having gotten used to them, have to depart again, but it is much better than having an "X" written on one's cage. Remember, if Mom had not come on August 13, I would have been put to sleep forever.

My shelter wants to build a better and bigger building as soon as possible. I want to help dogs in distress and I want to help my shelter to get a new building, even though I hated my stay there. I also want to help other shelters as long as my royalty money from Dara's Canine Foundation, Inc., lasts. I created the Foundation for this purpose.

Please help me to help shelters find a new family for every dog, although I am sure that no Mom will be as understanding and loving as mine.

Colophon

Dara, Autobiography of a Chesapeake Bay Retriever, *was
designed and set by Janin/Cliff Design, Inc. in Washington, D.C.
The type is Caslon throughout, the face begun in 1725
by William Caslon, the first English type-founder.
The pencil drawings are by Cole Johnson,
the photographs by Linda Rosenthal.
The first edition was printed by McNaughton & Gunn, Inc..*

*Dara, the Chesapeake Bay Retriever and autobiographer,
relates that she was born in the lap of luxury before
undertaking the remarkable and nearly fatal odyssey
recounted in these pages. Rescued in 1991 by the woman
who became her protector and amanuensis, Dara now divides
her time between homes in Maryland and rural Vermont.
Her dramatic story reveals the mind, soul and motives
of a magnificent dog whose humanity and largeness
of spirit will warm the hearts of readers of all ages.*

*Lolo Sarnoff, Dara's Mom and collaborator, is a sculptor
and founder-president of Arts for the Aging, Inc., (AFTA),
a not-for-profit organization dedicated to teaching
the arts in senior daycare centers. Previously she assisted
her husband, the late Stanley J. Sarnoff, M.D.
and co-authored many medical papers with him.*